Tarquin the Wonder Horse

Tarquin
the
Wonder
Horse

June Crebbin
Illustrated by Tony Ross

WALKER
BOOKS

For Gail and David
and
Somerby Equestrian Centre

First published 2000 by Walker Books Ltd
87 Vauxhall Walk, London SE11 5HJ

This edition published 2017

2 4 6 8 10 9 7 5 3 1

Text © 2000 June Crebbin
Illustrations © 2000 Tony Ross

The right of June Crebbin and Tony Ross to be identified as author
and illustrator respectively of this work has been asserted by them
in accordance with the Copyright, Designs and Patents Act 1988

This book has been typeset in Garamond

Printed in Great Britain by Clays Ltd, St Ives plc

British Library Cataloguing in Publication Data:
a catalogue record for this book is available from the British Library

ISBN 978-1-4063-7873-3

www.walker.co.uk

Contents

Chapter One

Once, a horse, weary of travelling in far-off countries, decided to return home. As his ship pulled into the harbour, he thought, the first thing I must do is find a job. But I'll say nothing of my magic powers. They only bring trouble.

Still, he decided to use his power of speech.

In the market he approached a farmer. "Are you looking for a good, strong worker?" he asked.

The farmer, though extremely
surprised to hear the horse speak,
knew a bargain when he saw one
and hired him on the spot.

Tarquin, that was the horse's name, settled quickly into his new home. His workday was long and hard. But in the quiet evenings, he enjoyed the company of a grey mouse. She told him about the fat farm cat and its attempts to catch her.

12

"Mind you," said the mouse, "I don't go in the house. I'm not stupid. Though sometimes, I can't help wishing for a piece of cheese."

And that's when Tarquin should have kept quiet.

Outside, the farmer, who was passing by, heard him say: "I can grant your wish. Take hold of a single strand of my mane, pull it out and speak your heart's desire. Be careful not to *break* the strand, or the magic will be undone."

Well, the mouse nipped up
Tarquin's leg, took hold of a single
strand of mane – and pulled.

At once, the hair changed into a
chunk of cheese.

"There's plenty more where that
came from!" laughed Tarquin.

The farmer trembled with excitement.

More where that came from? he thought. I should say! I could wish for gold. A gold piece for every strand! But I must think carefully. That horse is strong and he might not want to give up *all* his mane.

He hurried into the farmhouse.

Some time later, a smile spread across his face.

Chapter Two

Early next morning, the farmer mixed some special herbs into Tarquin's food.

When Tarquin ate breakfast he began to feel sleepy and soon he slumped to the floor.

The farmer brought a sack, put on thick gloves, and pulled and pulled until Tarquin's whole mane was his.

Laughing, he carried it into the farmhouse.

He took hold of a single strand of hair. "I wish for a piece of gold!" he cried.

At once the hair changed into a gold piece.

The farmer grabbed a handful of hair. "I wish for ten pieces of gold for every strand!" he shouted.

At once, gold pieces filled his hands.

The farmer shook with excitement. He grabbed up the rest of the mane in his arms.

"I wish for a thousand – no, a MILLION – pieces of gold for every strand!" he yelled.

At once, gold pieces appeared
all over the kitchen. Like drops of
golden rain, they poured down onto
the floor. The farmer scooped them
up in his hands. He let them trickle
like water through his fingers.

"I'm rich! I'm rich!" he cried.

The gold kept coming.

The farmer was up to his knees –

"All mine!" he shouted.

The gold rose higher. Now the farmer was up to his waist ... his chest –

"That's enough!" he protested, laughing. "Stop! Stop!"

The farmer could hardly breathe.
The gold was crushing him.

He tried to think. There'd been a
warning. Something the horse had
said... "Be careful not to *break* the
strand..."

The farmer noticed one last strand of hair that he had missed before. He managed to reach it, and quickly pulled it in two.

At once, the kitchen fell silent. Even the birds outside stopped singing. When they started again a moment later, all the gold had gone.

All day, Tarquin lay in a deep sleep.
At last, towards evening, he stirred.

The mouse crept from her corner.

Tarquin lifted his head. His neck felt
strangely light.

"The farmer took your mane," the
mouse told him. "He must know of
your magic."

"Then I cannot stay," said Tarquin.

Sadly, he said goodbye to his friend,
left the farm and set out on his travels
once more.

Chapter Three

Snow began to fall as Tarquin left the village. Soon it was difficult to see where he was going.

That night, he huddled by a hedge.

The next morning, the snow had stopped but the road was icy and since there was no one about, Tarquin drew in his breath – and blew.

Out of his nostrils shot twin blasts of fire. At once, the ice in front of him melted. Tarquin stepped forward eagerly. Surely he would find a friendly farmhouse soon?

High on the crest of a hill, a
woman was watching Tarquin's
fiery progress. She was Gelda, the
Queen's cousin, out hunting the
rare snow eagle.

"A fire-breathing horse!" she
murmured excitedly.

She gave her huntsmen orders to abandon the search for the snow eagle, and capture the horse instead. "Be careful!" she snapped. "I don't want him frightened." Then she sped back to her palace.

"Prepare the Master Stable!" she ordered. "Put out the golden hay net, but bring the silver drinking bucket to me."

Chapter Four

So Tarquin awoke the next morning
not in a farmhouse, but in a royal
palace. He was taken to Gelda,
where a silver bucket was placed
before him. He was desperate for
a drink.

But the bucket was full of ice.

"How am I to drink this?" he asked.

"Oh, you can speak!" cried Gelda.

"I need water, not ice," said Tarquin. "Then *melt* it!" shrieked Gelda. "Like you melted it yesterday!" Tarquin's heart sank.

"Think of the posters!" cried Gelda. "IS IT A HORSE OR IS IT A DRAGON? COME AND SEE THE ONLY FIRE-BREATHING HORSE IN THE WORLD! Two shows nightly."

"No, thank you," said Tarquin.

He turned to leave.

"Stop him!" yelled Gelda.

Tarquin felt the points of a dozen deadly swords.

"It wouldn't be safe," he warned. "Things could go wrong."

Chapter Five

At seven o'clock that night, the crowds assembled in the Palace Theatre. The band, sitting just in front of the stage, played a few rousing marches. Then the announcer cried: "Ladies and Gentlemen, allow me to introduce Tarquin – the Dragon Horse!"

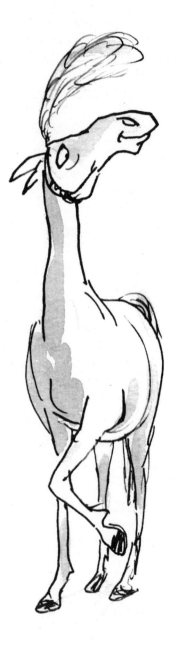

On came Tarquin, with a plume on his head and his hooves painted gold.

The announcer stood up.

"First," he cried, "Tarquin will light the birthday candles!"

On to the stage came a small girl carrying a cake with six candles. She placed it on a table and stood back.

Tarquin drew in his breath.

He blew – very, very gently.

All six candles lit.

The crowd cheered.

Next, five unlit torches were brought on, each in its own stand.

Tarquin drew in his breath. He blew – not quite so gently this time.

All five torches lit.

The crowd roared.

"And finally!" cried the announcer.
"The Leap of Fire! Not only will
Tarquin light the hoop, he will then
leap through it!"

The crowd quietened.

An enormous hoop, covered
in paper, was brought on. The
drummers began their drum roll.

Tarquin drew in his breath. He
blew – hard and long.

Twin blasts of fire shot straight
through the hoop of paper to the very
edge of the stage. Flames licked the
sheets of music that the band was
playing. They caught alight.

"FIRE!" shouted the trumpeter.

"FIRE!" yelled the tuba player.

The Royal Fire Officers rushed in
with buckets and hoses.

Water gushed everywhere. Hats
were soaked, dresses drenched,
trousers sodden.

Every time Gelda opened her

mouth to scream an order, she got a
jet of water in it.

Showers bounced off drums.
Flutes spurted fountains. The tuba
filled up like a giant teacup.

Tarquin quietly made his way
down the back stairs, out of the
palace and into the night.

Chapter Six

That's it, thought Tarquin. No more getting mixed up with *people*.

He spent that night in the middle of a forest. It was very cold. But in the morning he woke to bright sunshine and the snow was melting fast.

He stretched. It was lovely to feel the warmth on his back.

"Oh, what a beautiful morning!" he sang, going to drink at a nearby stream. "Oh, what a beautiful day!"

The water tasted good.

Behind him, a twig broke. He swung round.

A girl stared. Then from behind the trees, a boy appeared.

The girl said, "I'm Rosanna. He's Paul.

Are you a magic horse?"

At once, Tarquin was on his guard.

"It's just that you have golden hooves," said Rosanna.

"And a splendid plume," said Paul. Tarquin snorted.

"And you sing beautifully!" said Rosanna. "So we thought you must be magic."

Tarquin pawed the ground. He remembered what he'd decided yesterday: *No more getting mixed up with people.* But these children didn't seem so bad.

"I'm Tarquin," he said.

"Please, we need your help," said Paul. He kept looking behind him.

For the first time, Tarquin noticed they were frightened.

Suddenly, there was a great roar.

SEVENTY-ONE SEVENTY-TWO I'M GETTING HUNGRY

The children clung
to each other.

"It's the Ogre!"
they sobbed.

"There isn't
much time," said
Rosanna urgently.
"We're supposed to
be hiding. The Ogre

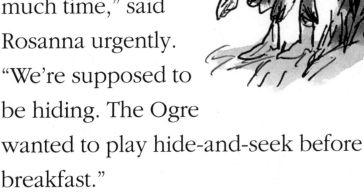

wanted to play hide-and-seek before
breakfast."

"That sounds fun!" said Tarquin.
"That's a good game!"

"It isn't!" cried Paul.

And then Tarquin realized – it
wasn't a game. The children were the
Ogre's breakfast.

NINETY-EIGHT NINETY-NINE A HUNDRED

"You could save us," begged Rosanna. "You could carry us away."

READY OR NOT!

roared the Ogre.

"He's coming! He's coming!"
screamed Paul.

Chapter Seven

"Jump on my back!" cried Tarquin.
Rosanna and Paul leapt up.

Just as the Ogre crashed into the
clearing, Tarquin was away.

Behind them came a howl of rage: "You won't get far!"

The Ogre set off after them, covering the ground in mighty strides.

"Faster! Faster!" urged Rosanna.

But Tarquin couldn't. The forest
was too thick. He had to look for
paths between the trees.

The Ogre was gaining on them.

If anything got in his way, he simply
struck it to one side.

Rosanna glanced behind. He was
almost on them. "Oh Tarquin, I *wish*
you could fly!" she cried.

At that moment, Tarquin swerved to avoid a rabbit hole. Rosanna clutched at his newly growing mane – and a single strand of hair came loose... Tarquin's shoulder muscles slowly rippled outwards, on and on, until they weren't muscles at all, but huge silver wings.

Up, up soared the horse and the
children, leaving the Ogre crashing
with anger below.

Over the forest they flew, and
away.

Rosanna leaned forward. "There!"
she cried. "Can you see? By the lake,
at the foot of the mountain. That's
our village."

As they flew closer, people came
running out to greet them.

Tarquin landed softly. The children tumbled off.

"Tarquin," whispered Rosanna, leading him forward to meet her family and friends, "you're a Wonder!"

Tarquin still lives in the village. He helps with the ploughing and the haymaking. He's a strong and willing worker, and he keeps the Ogre away. No one ever dreams of plucking out a strand of his mane.

Except the children, of course. Just now and then.

June Crebbin is the author of a number of books for children, including *Invasion*, a story about the Norman Conquest; *The Queen's Maid*, about a young girl working in the court of Queen Elizabeth I; four Merryfield Hall Riding School stories; and several picture books for younger children, including the bestselling *Cows in the Kitchen*, illustrated by Katharine McEwen. June has two grown-up sons and two grandsons and lives in Leicestershire.